In memory of my friend 'Phil' Mason

First published in Great Britain in 2000
First paperback publication in 2001
by ORCHARD BOOKS
96 Leonard Street, London EC2A 4XD
Orchard Books Australia
Unit 31/56 O'Riordan Street, Alexandria, NSW 2015
1 84121 205 9 (hardback)
1 84121 604 6 (paperback)
Copyright © Arthur Robins 2000
The right of Arthur Robins to be identified as the author and
illustrator of this work has been asserted by him in accordance
with the Copyright, Designs and Patents Act, 1988.
A CIP catalogue record for this book is available from the British Library.
2 4 6 8 10 9 7 5 3 1 (hardback)
2 4 6 8 10 9 7 5 3 1 (paperback)
Printed in Dubai

The Blacksmith and the Giant

ARTHUR ROBINS

ORCHARD BOOKS

The Blacksmith and the Giant

A long time ago, not far from here
lived Sam the Blacksmith.
Tap, tap, clink, clank, clank.
People would stop to watch when
they heard the sound of him working.

And as he worked he sang...
 "I might be thin,
I might be wiry,
but I can bend iron
that's hot and fiery.
I bash it like this,
and beat it like so.
Guess what I'm making –
does anyone know?

What *is* he making?

Sam and the people were ruled by a cruel king
and his rabble army of bullies and riff-raff.

On market day, they would march into town
singing their gruff marching song.

"Make way for the King! We won't pay for a thing.
We'll just help ourselves to cakes from your shelves,
and if you ask us for cash, we'll give you a bash!"

And they took whatever they wanted
without a 'please' or 'thank you'.

For the king and his thugs,

life couldn't have been more pleasant,

dining each day on lemonade and pheasant,

jelly, cakes and buns for tea.

They stuffed their faces, all for free.

Until one evening at a nearby stream,

the king's spy spotted some giant footprints.

"A giant!" screeched the king.
"Surely there's no such thing."
"But I saw him with my beady eye,"
said the king's snooping spy.

"I can't have a massive great lout, clomping about,
I must think of a way to keep him out!
A big fierce dog might do the trick
but he could turn friendly and just give him a lick.
Send for the blacksmith!" ordered the king.

"Smithy," said the king to Sam,
"what I need is a new pair of gates
high enough and strong enough
to keep out the fiercest of giants."
"I'm afraid I don't have enough
iron for such a huge task,"
said Sam, bowing extra low,
knowing he wouldn't get paid.

"Silence!" shrieked the king.
"You'll obey my wish
or I'll have your head on a silver dish.
I've been told there's a giant about
and I need strong gates to keep him out,
with locks and bolts to shut them tight
so I'll feel safe in my bed at night.
And if he tries to climb over the top,
something sharp to make him stop.

A nasty stab in his behind,

I think that should make him change his mind.

Good then, that's agreed.

My men will collect all the iron you need,

pots and pans, your granny's bed.

Now get to work, or lose your head!"

So Sam worked day and night
bashing away with big hammers,
and tapping with smaller ones.
Heating, beating, banging and clanging
the iron into shape.
But this time, no one came to watch,
and Sam didn't sing.

Weeks later, the gates were ready.
The band played, the king waved,
and the people booed (quietly).
Sam slipped away before
the crowd turned nasty.

As he made his way home, suddenly from out of the sky,
a very large belt buckle dropped right in front of him.

Sam fell back in fright, and standing over him
was a gigantic, gruesome, grinning giant.
"D...d...don't eat me!" squeaked Sam.
"Eat you?" the giant roared with laughter. "I'd
sooner eat my toenails!" and laughed so much...

…his trousers fell down!

"Oh my goodness," said the giant. "How embarrassing!"
and went quite red.

"I…I…I could fix that for you," said Sam shaking.

"Could you?" said the giant. "It's my favourite belt.
I've had it since I was only twenty feet high."

Back at the smithy, the giant watched
as Sam started to repair the belt and as he worked,
he nervously began to sing.

"I'll give the buckle a little tap
and fix it for this enormous chap.
For a giant is a terrifying sight
and without trousers can give you quite a fright."

"It's as good as new! I'm so pleased. I must repay you somehow," the giant said.

"There is something," said Sam, feeling a little braver.

"At your service," boomed the giant.

And Sam told him how the king had taken everyone's baths and things and hadn't paid him for his work.

"Show me the way," growled the giant.

"We'll give him a fright."

"Open up!" boomed the giant. "You owe money!
I'm here to collect!"

"Go away!" yelled the king, who was playing
with his gold. "You've made me lose count!"

"Squash him!" shouted Sam. "Tear down the gates!"

"Squash him?" said the giant crossly. "I'm not a hooligan. We'll
send him a bill."

"What's this!" bellowed the king who had never seen a
bill before. He began to read it. "For services rendered…
what services is the big lump offering?
Blocking out the sunlight, ha, ha, ha!"

And all his men laughed. "Ha, ha, ha."

"Go away!" yelled the king, tearing up the bill.
"You're not getting your hands on my gold!"
And he started to swallow it,
helping it down with great
swigs of fizzy lemonade.

Gulp, splosh, burp!

A handful of gold,
and another big slurp.
"I'm not giving my gold
to that overgrown twerp."
After a while he
began to feel funny,
as the fizzy lemonade
swelled up in his tummy.
Then without a sound,
his feet left the ground
and he floated across the room,
like an enormous balloon.

"I can fly! You can't get me!" he called down
to the amazed giant and crowd...

POP!

...and flew straight onto the gates.

The crowd were showered with gold.

"Hurrah for the giant! Sam for King!"
the people cheered.

"Please stay," said Sam to the giant.
"You could do all the castle bills,
and be the chief gatekeeper."

Now that he was king, Sam made
baths, kettles and bedsteads from all
the armour and swords left behind.
    And all the people came to watch,
including the giant. Like everyone else,
he loved to guess what Sam would make next.